Dear Parent:

Congratulations! Your child is taking the first steps on an exciting journey. The destination? Independent reading!

STEP INTO READING® will help your child get there. The program offers five steps to reading success. Each step includes fun stories and colorful art. There are also Step into Reading Sticker Books, Step into Reading Math Readers, Step into Reading Write-In Readers, Step into Reading Phonics Readers, and Step into Reading Phonics First Steps! Boxed Sets—a complete literacy program with something for every child.

Learning to Read, Step by Step!

Ready to Read   Preschool–Kindergarten
• **big type and easy words** • **rhyme and rhythm** • **picture clues**
For children who know the alphabet and are eager to begin reading.

Reading with Help   Preschool–Grade 1
• **basic vocabulary** • **short sentences** • **simple stories**
For children who recognize familiar words and sound out new words with help.

Reading on Your Own   Grades 1–3
• **engaging characters** • **easy-to-follow plots** • **popular topics**
For children who are ready to read on their own.

Reading Paragraphs   Grades 2–3
• **challenging vocabulary** • **short paragraphs** • **exciting stories**
For newly independent readers who read simple sentences with confidence.

Ready for Chapters   Grades 2–4
• **chapters** • **longer paragraphs** • **full-color art**
For children who want to take the plunge into chapter books but still like colorful pictures.

STEP INTO READING® is designed to give every child a successful reading experience. The grade levels are only guides. Children can progress through the steps at their own speed, developing confidence in their reading, no matter what their grade.

Remember, a lifetime love of reading starts with a single step!

For my family—K.H.

Step into Reading, Random House, and the Random House colophon are registered trademarks of Random House, Inc.

Visit us on the Web!
www.stepintoreading.com
www.randomhouse.com/kids

Educators and librarians, for a variety of teaching tools, visit us at
www.randomhouse.com/teachers

Library of Congress Cataloging-in-Publication Data
Hammond, Katie.
BURN·E the fix-it bot / by Katie Hammond ; inspired by the art and character designs created by Pixar.
    p. cm.
"WALL·E."
ISBN 978-0-7364-2609-1 (trade) — ISBN 978-0-7364-8070-3 (lib. bdg.)
I. Pixar (Firm) II. WALL·E (Motion picture) III. Title.
PZ7.H18456Bu 2009
[E] —dc22   2008032568

Printed in the United States of America   10 9 8 7 6 5 4 3 2 1   First Edition

Disney · PIXAR

WALL·E

By Katie Hammond

Inspired by the art and

character designs created by Pixar

WITHDRAWN

Random House 🏠 New York

The AXIOM is
a big spaceship.

Robots do everything
on the ship.

This is BURN•E.

He repairs the ship.

This is SUPPLY•R.

He gives out extra parts.

Uh-oh!

A light broke!

BURN•E can fix it.

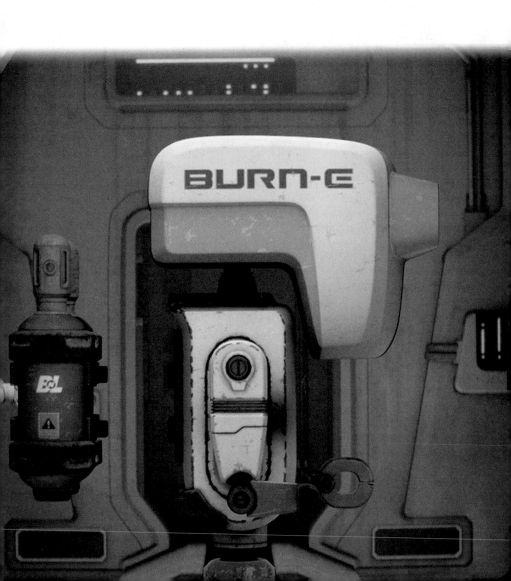

SUPPLY•R gives BURN•E

a new light.

BURN•E starts to fix

the broken light.

WALL•E rides by.

He waves.

BURN•E waves back.

The light floats away.

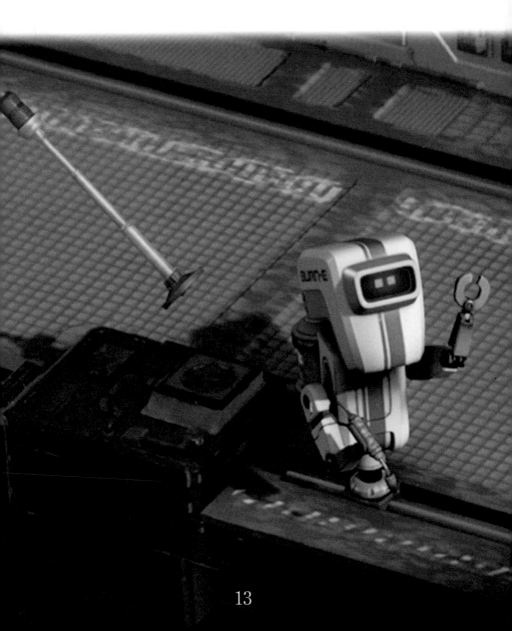

BURN•E goes to SUPPLY•R.

He gets a new light.

BURN•E will try again.

The light is up!

BURN•E is not done yet.

BURN•E has to go back in.

He must turn it on.

Someone has closed the door.

BURN•E is locked out!

BURN•E looks for a way in.

He sees an open door!

A bot named WALL•A closes the door.

Will BURN•E
make it inside?

BURN•E was too slow.

The door is closed.

BURN•E gets an idea!

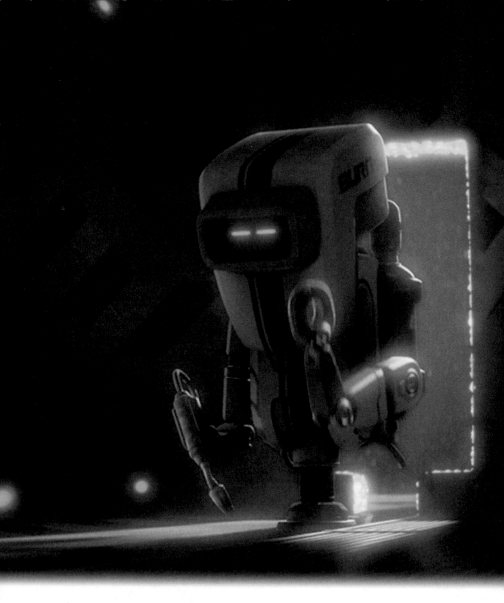

BURN•E makes
his own door.

The AXIOM speeds up!

It is flying to Earth.

BURN·E holds on!

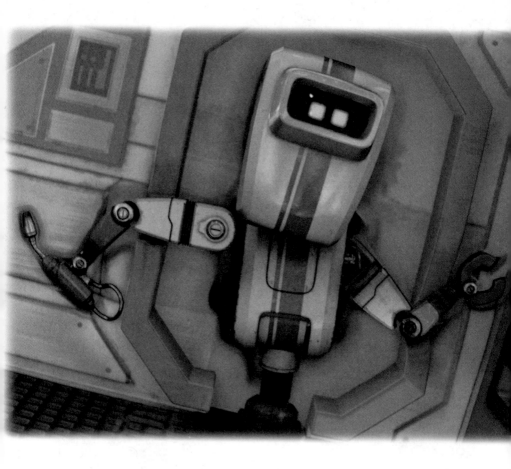

He gets in a life pod.

It heads to Earth!

It lands.

He sees the other bots.

BURN•E sees the light.

Will it turn on?

Hooray! It works!
Great job, BURN•E!

Oh, no!

The light breaks again!

Back to work, BURN•E!